INSPIRING TRUE STORIES BOOK FOR 8 YEAR OLD BOYS

I AM 8
AND
AMAZING

Inspirational tales About Courage, Self-Confidence and Friendship

Paula Collins

Contents

Introduction

Hello, intrepid and wonderful boy! Did you know that you are exceptional? You are unique in the entire universe, which means there is no one like you in this vast world. That's truly amazing! Among billions of people, you have a special way of facing life. You are brave, funny, intelligent, and incredible. Never forget that.

In the world, you will find challenges of all sizes. Some may scare you, while others may make you doubt yourself. But remember, we all feel these emotions. Your parents, siblings, grandparents, friends, and even strangers feel the same as you.

Even when you face your fears, remember that you can overcome them and grow. When trying something new or facing difficult situations, you may feel fear at first, but the experiences that scare you the most often turn out to be the most valuable. Learn from your mistakes and find the goodness in everything you do, even when things are harder than you imagined.

In this book, you will find stories of children like you, brave and strong, who face situations similar to yours every day. They also feel fear and worry and sometimes don't win, but they work hard, keep trying, and learn from their mistakes until they achieve their goals.

When they feel discouraged or begin to doubt themselves, these children find that unique light within them that helps them keep going, even when they think about giving up. In each story, these children discover self-confidence, hope, and courage that allow them to live incredible experiences in every situation, leading them to reach their dreams.

Now is the time to light up your corner of the world. Share your light with others, free yourself from fear, and learn life's lessons. Believe in yourself, and you can accomplish anything.

You are an amazing and unique boy!

Grandpa's Piano

Do you ever wonder what you want to be when you grow up? A doctor, a teacher, a soccer player, a painter, or maybe a singer? It's okay to not know yet. Just try out different things and see what makes your heart happy. Let's read about Ethan, a boy who was looking for what he loved to do.

Ethan is a curious boy who loves discovering new things. He lives with his mom, dad, big brother, and little sister. He's always asking questions because he

wants to learn. In Ethan's family, everyone has something they really love doing. His mom is a nurse who loves helping people. His dad is a lawyer who solves problems. His big brother enjoys painting and has made the house look beautiful with his art. His little sister is great at soccer and even scores goals for her team at school.

Everyone in Ethan's family loves what they do. Ethan has tried things like dancing, singing, and drawing, but he often gets bored. One night, he was lying in bed, wondering what special thing he would love to do every day. Thinking about it made him excited, and soon he fell asleep. When he woke up the next morning, he was ready to discover his own special passion.

Ethan quickly put on his clothes and joined his family for breakfast.

While munching on his cereal, he asked his mom, "Mom, can you help me find something fun and special to do today? I want to find what I love, just like you and dad."

His mom smiled and said, "How about coming with me to the hospital today? You might find something you like there.

Ethan went with his mom to the hospital where she worked, but he got really scared when he saw a tiny bit of blood.

So, his mom said, "Why not try painting like your brother? Or play soccer like your sister?"

With his brother's help, Ethan painted a picture. Later, he played soccer with his sister in the park. But neither felt right for him.

The next day, he watched what his dad did, but it seemed boring. His mom suggested different sports like basketball, swimming, and even skating at the park. But Ethan just didn't enjoy any of them.

Ethan felt like everything was just boring.

He sighed, thinking, "Will I ever find something I love to do every single day?" He was starting to lose hope.

One day, during a visit to his grandpa's house, Ethan's curiosity led him to the attic. There, he spotted a big, dusty piano. It looked old but special.

Excitedly, Ethan raced to find his grandpa and said, "Grandpa! There's a cool piano in the attic! Can I try to fix it and play it?"

Grandpa looked thoughtful and replied, "Oh, that old thing? That piano belonged to my dad. It's very old,

Ethan. I'm not sure it can be fixed, and it might be too costly." He paused and added, "It's been up there so long; I doubt it would make any sound now."

Ethan wasn't ready to give up on the piano.

He turned to his dad and said, "Dad, can we find someone to fix the piano?" Knowing how important it was to Ethan, his dad decided to help. He remembered an old friend who played the piano and thought he might have some advice.

When the pianist friend saw the old instrument in the attic, his eyes lit up.

"This piano is special," he said. "I think we can find someone to bring it back to life!"

Ethan's face glowed with happiness. He hugged his dad tightly and exclaimed, "Thanks, Dad! I really want to play it. I can't wait!"

A couple of weeks later, the piano was back at Ethan's house, looking as good as new. Ethan was so excited that he invited his friends over to listen to the first notes under his fingers. With a big smile, he took a seat and started to play. But, oops! The notes sounded a bit funny.

When he attempted his first little tune, one friend giggled, and soon the whole room was filled with laughter.

Ethan's cheeks turned red, and he felt a bit embarrassed. He had hoped to impress his friends, but things didn't go as planned.

Ethan felt really sad and ran to his room with tears in his eyes.

"I thought playing would be simple," he said with a sniffle, "Maybe I'm not good at anything."

But Mom and Dad wanted to help. They got him a special app on his tablet to learn piano. Ethan tried and practiced every day and night for a whole week.

The next Saturday was his sister Lily's birthday. Mom and Dad wanted Ethan to play the piano for everyone.

"But Mom," Ethan said, "I don't want my friends to laugh at me again. It hurt my feelings."

His mom smiled kindly and said, "Ethan, you've worked so hard and practiced a lot. I believe in you. Just believe in yourself too."

Ethan took a deep breath and began to play the songs he had learned. To his surprise, everyone was

impressed! They clapped and cheered for him. Ethan's heart swelled with pride.

Seeing how much he loved the piano, his mom arranged for a teacher to give him lessons. Every day, after school, Ethan practiced. He got better and better, and his love for music grew.

A few months later, Ethan was invited to play at a big recital in the city. He was so nervous at first, but as he played, his confidence grew. The music flowed beautifully from his fingers. At the end of the show, he received a special prize for his amazing performance.

From that day on, Ethan knew he had found his true passion: playing the piano. And his favorite piano? It was always Grandpa's!

Ethan discovered that finding his passion meant trying different things, even if it was tough. Even when he faced challenges, or when others doubted him, he never gave up. He learned that to be good at something, you have to practice and give it your all. And when you finally find what you love, share it with the world. Just like Ethan, always chase your dreams and never give up on finding what makes you happy.

You're one of a kind, a special boy unlike any other. It's okay to take your time to discover what you truly love. Always listen to your heart and stay true to yourself. No matter what, know that you are incredible just the way you are.

Rising Through the Ranks

Have you ever been chosen for something you don't like? Have you felt that your talent is not valued? This is a story where a boy is not chosen for the position he wants, but it is just a stepping stone in his growth.

His desire to be part of the team was evident since he was old enough to be enrolled in the city team. Ethan has wanted to be a soccer player since he was a little boy. When he was just a baby, he would take a ball and start kicking it against a wall. He soon

learned that when he kicked it, it would come back, then he would move to the side and stop it to kick it again.

As he grew older and his legs became stronger and more agile, he began to do other things. He self-taught himself to bounce it on his knee, kick it in different poses, and even do pirouettes.

In his town, kids had to be eight years old to join the soccer team. He had been waiting since he was seven! He even reminded his dad that right after his eighth birthday, they should go sign up. He was so excited for his birthday. And right after turning eight, he found the flyer with all the sign-up details. He was so happy! His dad promised to take him right away so he wouldn't miss out.

Ethan, not wanting to be left out, went to the playground with his ball and spent the rest of the day practicing. He made different pirouettes, bounces, jumps, and movements and played games on the internet, watching every play. He even read "Tips for a Soccer Tryout." He did not want to miss any detail on the day of the tryout and be disqualified, feeling sorry for himself and also sorry for what his father might think.

The night before the tryout, he was very excited. He prepared everything, chose the best sports clothes, cleaned the sports shoes with great care, and waited so that he would not miss any detail.

When he had everything ready, he went to bed. He wanted to rest well to be fresh the next day.

His parents were so proud. He had been very focused and disciplined, especially for a kid his age. They knew he really wanted to be on the team.

"It's time, son," his dad said as he walked into the room. But he was surprised to see his son already dressed and waiting, ready to go.

After eating breakfast, they headed to the stadium for the tryouts. There were many boys and girls there, all hoping to get on the teams. Ethan knew he had to try his best if he wanted to make the team.

At the soccer fields, parents sat in the stands while the kids went to their spots. Boys on one field, and girls on another. They would try out one by one or in groups, depending on what the coaches wanted.

Over a hundred boys, including Ethan, hoped to join the team. But they were only picking up three new players that year. The city's team was one of the best, so everyone wanted to be a part of it.

Right away, Ethan started to feel nervous and sweaty. He really didn't want to hear his name when the coaches began picking who would stay and who would go. Even though he thought he did well in each drill, he saw other good players being told to leave.

From the big group of about a hundred boys, soon only 30 were left. The drills got tougher, but Ethan still did them with ease, moving around the field without trouble.

When only 20 boys remained, they stood in a big circle with the coach in the middle. The coach had them practice passing the ball and trying to take it from one another.

Everyone tried their best, making fancy moves and trying to keep the ball away, even from the coach. Some did great, but others got their feet mixed up or felt frustrated.

When Ethan's turn came, he had to try and get the ball from a coach that no one could get the ball from before. Ethan had been watching and thought he knew the coach's weak spot. But when he tried, the coach quickly moved the ball aside. Even though Ethan made a good move, the coach played with the ball between his legs, and Ethan couldn't get it.

After that round, Ethan was relieved because they didn't call his name to leave.

As the tryouts continued, the circle of boys got smaller and smaller until only a few were left. They had to run, dribble, and move all over the field. Ethan felt like he ran more than anyone.

Soon, only three boys remained, and Ethan was one of them. The coach began to say what position each boy would play. Ethan noticed the blonde boy he'd seen at the start had made it too. He was going to be a forward.

Ethan felt a bit sad. He really wanted to be a forward. Another boy, with shiny black hair and really dark eyes, who always smiled and showed bright white teeth, was picked to be the goalkeeper. He was super quick in the drills.

Then it was Ethan's turn. He was so surprised when the coach said he would be the referee!

They had also tested Ethan on soccer rules, and he knew them all. Plus, he could run all over the field and not get tired. But Ethan felt sad about being picked as the referee. He thought his dad would be disappointed too.

When Ethan walked over to his dad, he saw a big, proud smile on his dad's face.

"My son, you were among the three; congratulations, you are part of the selection."

"Well, yes, I am part of it," he said sadly.

"What's wrong? Wasn't that what you wanted?"

"I'm the referee."

The father was silent for a second, chewing on the information, and then grinned from ear to ear.

"That means you'll be at every game, even the ones that aren't with your team. Congratulations!"

His father then explained to him that it was part of growing up. Maybe right now he hadn't been chosen for the position he wanted, but he could keep applying and preparing. The referee position was very important, and we didn't pick just anyone.

Ethan knew that part of growing up and getting the position he wanted meant learning to take it one step at a time, even in those positions that at first you may not like very much or that aren't what you want. In time, Ethan would become one of the highest-scoring forwards on the team, making it to the national league.

Always give your best, and if you don't get chosen for what you want, you can always keep working for your dreams. Every step is valuable and necessary.

Learning to Follow the Rules

Have you ever gone to other houses and been given rules that you don't understand why they exist? Do you feel like breaking the rule you are being asked to follow? This story is about how a little boy understood that his uncle was right to ask him not to do something.

David's relationship with his uncle was strange because he saw him from time to time. He had excellent humor; they played, and he always told

some very funny jokes that made him laugh. He also had a strict side to his character. He said that he liked people to do things correctly and comply with the rules because that was how the world could function properly.

David was an 8-year-old boy. He was also a big fan of animals, especially dogs. He liked cats, but not as much.

One of the reasons why he liked to go to his uncle's place was because he had a dog named Olaf, a very playful German shepherd with whom he got along very well. They played, they chased each other, and he licked him until, in the end, he felt that all his skin smelled like dog, but he did not mind because he loved him very much.

Although his uncle was strict with the orders to the dog, they could only play in certain areas of the house; he could not take him to others, and they had time for play. He said:

"Dogs that are left too long on soft things like playing turn into kittens, and I want a dog to take care of them."

The uncle worked as a mechanic, and in the evenings, he would leave the dog inside the garage, next to the house, guarding it in case someone wanted to get in.

The German shepherd would bark at him, and he wouldn't dare.

The uncle had the idea that if Olaf played too much one night, instead of protecting the workshop, he would open it so that whoever wanted to enter would be able to get in comfortably and look for what he wanted to take.

The trips to his uncle's place happened from time to time. They lived in the same city, but from one end to the other. David's mother, his uncle's sister, was the one who took him every two weeks or once a month to visit and stay for a day.

That day of the visit, besides having Olaf in the back of the house, there was in the living room, on one of the pieces of furniture, an orange cat, asleep with its paws stretched out and deep.

"This one is as he wants to be," said David's mother to her son.

"What a comfort this cat is—lazy," said David.

"It's Luciano," said the uncle.

"He's been here for a few days."

"He's cute. Can I play with Olaf?" said David.

"Yes, but on one condition."

"Okay."

"You can't bring him into the house for anything."

"But this is where we always play."

"This time, it can't be because these two don't get along. They play in the workshop."

After they finished eating, David's mom left. She told him she'd be back soon and that he would stay with his uncle. She reminded David to be good and follow the house rules.

David resigned and went to the workshop. There was a big and badly parked truck, leaving a small space to play. When Olaf felt his friend nearby, he looked for play, and they chased each other several times around the truck.

David hit the bumper three times, and in some parts, he had to pass sideways because of the wall or the tool machine.

"My uncle didn't know how to park this," he said. "It's ugly to play like that."

David looked inside the house, but his uncle was not around. He saw Olaf and snapped his fingers to be

followed. The dog did not move. What he did was tilt his head with a questioning expression.

David looked at him again and said,

"Come, I permit you."

The dog, still hesitating, followed him, sniffing everything, feeling that he was not on his ground. When they reached the living room, the place where they usually played on previous trips, the dog stopped and put on an expression of anger.

Luciano, the cat, stood up, and all his hair stood on end.

Instantly, the dog went after the cat, and the cat went after him in a fit. The two began to chase each other, taking whatever they could find with them.

Ornaments fell to the floor, a small library with books fell, a car door was on one side, and it turned and hit the floor, and in less than a minute, the whole house was upside down.

David chased the dog, trying to stop it, and also the cat, but had no luck.

"What's going on here?" said the uncle, who appeared to be screaming.

He took three steps and grabbed Olaf by the leash, dragging him while he shouted furiously at the cat, who was watching him angrily from afar.

The uncle left the dog in the workshop and locked him up. Now his cold gaze fell on David.

"Remember I asked you not to let the dog in?"

David nodded ruefully.

"What was going to happen?"

"They were going to fight with the cat."

"That's right; you see what happened."

The uncle turned his back on him and went to the backyard, then came back with a broom, a mop, a bucket, and disinfectants.

"Do you see how wet the floor is?"

"Yes."

"The cat or the dog peed while fighting. You're going to clean it up and pick it up."

What took the dog and cat less than a minute to destroy took David two hours to pick up, tidy up, mop the floor, and clean thoroughly. He was sorry that his uncle was upset.

When he finished, the house was sparkling clean and didn't seem to have had room for a dog and cat fight.

The fear David had was that when his mother arrived, the uncle would accuse him, but he didn't. Maybe the lesson of having to clean the whole floor and tidy every corner without anyone's help had been enough.

He learned that he should not break the rules in someone else's house and that he had to be attentive to what his elders told him. If he was in someone else's house and they gave him an order not to touch or move the pet, even if it bothered him because he could not play well, he had to obey it because there was a reason for it.

The next time he went to his uncle's house, there were no cars, and he was able to play with Olaf all over the workshop, but he had to make sure he did not meet the cat.

Sometimes there are rules that we don't like, but we are in someone else's house, or an adult asks us to do them, and we must respect them. They have a reason for asking you not to do something. If you want to do it, ask permission first.

United We Stand

Have you ever worked in a team? Sometimes, everyone has different ideas, and it's tricky to decide together. But these stories will show how teams can work together and get great results!

Ethan belongs to a boys' soccer team where he has his three best friends, John, Andrew, and Liam. They

have a plan to make sure they win that season's competition. They had the responsibility to make sure they got the cup.

Ethan couldn't believe they would win it, as the team was still preparing and had many flaws. They had to make it happen, and even though the goalkeeper was not the best at covering goals, he thought that John, Andrew, and Liam had the role of putting together an offense and scoring goals.

Each of them had their own ideas of how to organize themselves.

John had a different idea of how they would play the next game.

Andrew also had a proposal for how they would organize the team.

Liam said they could stay as they were.

No one could agree, and tempers seemed to be heating up.

Ethan saw John and Andrew arguing. Liam was not around; apparently, he had left upset when no one heard him. Then he saw that he was having a conversation with the team manager and wondered what they were talking about.

Each person on the team was talking to the others, and then he noticed that Liam said goodbye to the director and seemed satisfied.

Liam came over and told everyone:

The director just told me that we should continue as we are, and he is the one who is in charge and recommends how we have to do things.

John looked at Liam and crossed his arms. He was furious, as he felt that he had acted on his own instead of deciding as a team.

He also felt the wrath of the team coming down on him, as he had brought the director in, so now they would have to stick to what they said and not negotiate.

"You should have talked to us before going to the big boss," Andrew said.

"But I wanted what was best for the team."

"Choosing for everyone?" said John.

"No one could agree."

"You could have been patient," said Ethan.

The three of them started to leave, and Liam refuted

"Where are they going?"

"We don't want to be with someone who doesn't know what teamwork is."

"We were fighting."

"We weren't. We were trying to find a balance and get on the same page."

Each one of them started talking at the same time, all giving their opinion, and no one was listening to each other. The only thing palpable there was the growing anger of all of them.

Ethan felt bad about what was happening. He was getting more frustrated with every minute they were arguing. He turned and saw John and Andrew standing next to him, talking as well. He realized that this fight he was in right now was only causing them to fight more and more.

Andrew saw and thought that his idea could be analyzed to see if they would reinforce it and do something between all of them to make it work better.

John thought almost the same thing. Since he could negotiate, it was still for the good of the team.

Liam thought that he had been very impulsive in going to the director to complain and ask them to continue as they were.

"I want us to propose something different," said Ethan, "but John refuted and gave me no chance; Liam went to accuse us; and Andrew also jumped on me."

All three looked uncomfortable.

"I don't want to work with Liam. He should even leave the team," said Andrew, "and accusing us in that way is not for friends."

"I didn't accuse them. I only proposed to continue as we were."

"You affected us anyway," said John.

Liam felt that he could have done things differently, but he didn't want to admit it.

The technical director intervened and watched silently as they all argued. Then he took out his whistle and blew it loudly, and they all fell silent.

"Andrew and John, do you have your proposals on the field?"

"That's right, director."

"Liam, do you want us to continue as we are and practice more so we can win the season?"

"Yes."

"Ethan, what do you want?"

"I don't even know. Right now, I just don't want to talk anymore."

"I don't think any of them have done things the way they should be done."

"I'm looking forward to winning this season," said Ethan, "but as it is, I doubt we'll be a laughing stock."

"Why don't you get together in pairs and start creating strategies? Then we'll discuss them and choose one that will help the whole team."

Ethan and Liam nodded, and John and Andrew agreed. They would make two groups each.

The director looked at the boys, and after reflecting for a while, he finally commented:

"What I want is for you to learn to work together. Both of you will continue to build a strategy that will help us reach the end of the season and win the cup."

"But we can't reach an agreement. We have been fighting for hours," said John.

"That's because none of you thought about what was best for the team."

They all felt uncomfortable, and so they have to figure out how they can have a single strategy.

Now they had to figure out how they could agree. If they didn't, they would ruin the future of the team.

The director walked away and said nothing more.

All the boys were silent, with a lot of feelings in the background, thinking about what would come next.

"What I did was not right," said Liam.

"It wasn't," said John.

The others nodded.

"At least we agree on one thing," then.

"I doubt this will work. I don't think we'll agree on the rest." said Andrew.

"Neither do I," said Ethan.

Liam sighed and, after a pause, said:

"Well, let's get down to strategizing."

They all went quietly to the big table area, where they discussed their moves and began to devise plans.

"I think we can combine my strategy of positioning ourselves in the position of the players on the field, surprising the other team," said John, "but we can combine it with what Andrew said, which is good too. The defense is stronger."

"I like the idea," said Ethan.

The boys put aside the annoyance that had been overwhelming them for hours, and now they were talking passionately, thinking about how they could win, comparing with the other teams, and knowing that with what was coming their way, the best strategy was to attack in one way or another.

Occasionally, when he disagreed, he would correct him by saying something positive first, like:

"That's a good strategy, but remember that the team's striker has a very strong left."

After this, Andrew and John became even closer friends than they already were, and Liam and Ethan also became great friends.

They understood that working as a team, although it was not always a garden of roses, if you respected each other, you could get the best result. They also discovered that they had a lot in common, so much

so that when they played the next game, they won two to zero and celebrated in style.

In the end, they didn't win the cup, but they made it to the final, which showed them that by working as a team, they could do better.

Working as a team, they found that they could achieve great things, and now they have managed over time to be better at what they did—winning championships and positioning themselves. Teamwork is like a group of gears that go in sync.

You don't have to do things alone. Every person in the world may have similar or different thoughts. They have a reason to think that way. You must respect their opinions and not offend them by trying to impose yours.

Sometimes there may be differences and different ways of doing things. Remember that each person's ideas are important, and find a way to work together and listen to opinions as much as possible. It will be helpful to have great experiences.

Learn to work as a team to achieve better results in what you propose, and respect the opinions that do not go with you.

Breaking the Ice

Have you ever wondered what it's like to be adopted? Every adopted child has a unique story. Sometimes, they build protective walls around themselves. Let's discover this story together.

For many months, it had been the topic that ran through the whole family. The word adoption was the word that was uttered most often in the day. Although at first Liam thought it was a bad idea, as

the months went by, he also became excited with each step they took to get permission to adopt a boy his age at home. Several times a visitor talked to Liam to find out how he was living at home; psychologists interviewed him, and they all wrote a lot in their notebooks.

He later learned that it was to see if his parents were fit to be parents.

They were because, finally, after so much effort, he would have a new brother who, to his good fortune, was his age.

"Let's go! Let's go get your brother. We have to be there at 10," said his father as he took the car keys and left.

His mother came out shortly after and was carrying things to welcome him. She was busy and wanted to show everything to her new son to make an excellent first impression.

"Come on, don't just stand there. Will you pick out a toy car to show your brother as a welcome?"

Liam thought that he could indeed look for a gift for his brother; a toy car would be ideal, but what would be his favorite kind of toy car, maybe a red race car?

Everyone loves race cars, and he had an awesome red toy car that he would like.

They started their journey. The orphanage where they would look for their new brother was on the outskirts of the city, so they all anxiously went through the town until they reached a country area and finally saw in the distance a huge house that looked like a castle to Liam.

"That's the one," said the father, pointing with his finger while holding the steering wheel.

When they arrived, a lady was waiting for them. They later learned that she was the headmistress. So they all passed by, the father chatting with her, the mother with some bags carrying many things for the boy, and Liam with the toy car.

They arrived at a special area where everyone would meet and go home with the new brother.

Liam was super excited to meet his new brother. He had imagined their first meeting so many times. How they would say hello, how they would quickly become friends, and even the silly arguments they might have. But when he finally saw his new brother, he was so surprised that he didn't know what to say or do.

In the living room, sitting with his arms crossed, an old shirt, and his head nailed to the floor, was a boy who was about his height and had a hard look as if he were angry.

When the headmistress approached, the boy looked at her with frightened and questioning eyes.

This is your new family, and you will be going with them.

The mother approached, knelt, and greeted him gently.

The boy seemed to sink deeper into himself.

The father came closer, and the boy made more of a scared face. He didn't like him.

They lasted a while, making contact, and then Liam slowly moved closer. He stood next to the boy, whom he knew was named Max. The boy saw him with a hard look. It seemed as if he was upset and felt his elusiveness, as if he didn't want him to look at him or talk to him.

They spent a few hours under the supervision of the headmistress, and then she approved for everyone to leave after the parents signed more papers and received another set of documents.

In the car, Max was sitting almost glued to the door, looking at his feet. Liam was very tense. He saw his new brother as if he were made of ice; he didn't want to talk, and it seemed that he was being taken to a catastrophic fate and not to a new home.

The toy car that had been there, ready to be used with his new brother, was resting on the seat. He hadn't even looked at it.

Liam just wanted it to be swallowed up by the earth. He hadn't imagined that this was how he would meet his new brother. Even in his more dramatic moments, he imagined he had a bigger brother controlling him but then dismissed the idea.

Once at home, they took Max to his room, left him food on the bedside table because he did not want to eat, and stayed locked up.

His parents told him that it was part of the process, that he had to adapt, and that the boy had been through a lot, and that was why he behaved like that, but that little by little, they would break that shell and discover the wonderful being that was hiding underneath, and that he should be patient.

The days passed, and Max barely responded with monosyllables and watched his brother with caution, as if waiting for some reaction from him, as if he was

going to attack him. Then, one day, Liam, exhausted from waiting for an approach, walked to his brother's room and entered unannounced. Max stood up from the bed and jumped back, leaning against the wall as if hoping to defend himself.

"It's all right; I won't do anything to you."

"Hello," said Max after a while.

"Why are you like this with me and with us? We just want to love you."

"It's not my first home. I don't want to get my hopes up," said Max.

"If you want, I promise you that this will be your final home. My parents are the most loving in the world, and that's why they chose to have you at home. They want to take care of you as they take care of me. So if you give them a chance, they will love you. If you give me a chance, I could love you as my brother."

"I have not been a big fan of my siblings. They don't treat me well."

"I did want you to come home, so you can always count on me."

Max began to relax, got off the bed, sat down, sat quietly for a minute, and then asked:

"Do you still have that toy car that I think you were going to give me the day we met?"

Liam nodded his head and ran off to his room, came back, and brought him the toy car; from that day on, they became inseparable, and soon after, Max behaved like one of the others at home. He blended in and had the opportunity to finish enjoying a happy childhood.

Maybe what Max needed was for someone to approach him in a friendly way at home. Mom and dad had only put food on him and talked to him, but as adults, they were not able to connect with him. It would be Liam who would show equal respect and manage to break through that wall. Liam began to introduce everyone to his brother, and wherever he went, he said he was his brother. Soon, no one would know if he was born or adopted. The truth did not matter because of the love they felt in that home.

For the social worker who did the monthly check-ups, and any day she was surprised, it was a great pleasure to see how the boy had adapted well and smiled happily to have parents who loved him and gave him what he had longed for so much. Liam soon had his brother in the same classroom. They each made groups of friends and shared, and sometimes they fought. Not everything was perfect, but come

on, after all, they were brothers. A little fight over who gets the toy or the pencil is typical in any good home.

Liam realized that every child has their own story. Maybe his brother had been through tough times that made him build a protective shield around himself. Some kids, like Max, face challenges at home or with families that don't understand them. But with love and patience, the true heart of a child can shine through.

Adopted children might have faced difficult times, but with understanding and care, they can feel loved and accepted.

.

A Slam Dunk Surprise game

Have you ever had to go somewhere you didn't really want to? Or do something that seemed boring at first? Sometimes, the things we least want to do can turn out to be the most fun of all! This story is about how playing a sport opened up a world full of exciting chances for our hero.

"Let's go; we have to be on time," said Sam's mother as she picked up her purse and took her bag.

It was a summer day when the sky was completely blue and cloudless.

His sister was a great basketball player, and he also liked the sport. They were always practicing baskets in the backyard.

He remembered that that day they would go with his mother and sister to the basketball practice she had in the city. This was a practice that only stopped on vacations; usually, Sam never went, but since dad wasn't there, he had to go with them.

"I don't feel like going, mom; I promise I'll be good."

The mother was firm. He had to go, whether he liked it or not.

"We already talked about it, son; you have to go. It won't take long. You'll have a good time."

Sam knew he had no way out. He had to go with his mother; he had never won this kind of discussion. He preferred to stay and play or color, but not to go to a court to see his sister with a ball.

He put his head down, looked at the ground, and resignedly accepted his fate.

His sister Nat tried to cheer him up and said,

"You'll see that basketball is fun. I have a great time with my friends. I'm sure you'll like it if you try it."

He preferred to play at home, not go out. He didn't understand those girls with a ball on an indoor court.

When they arrived, he noticed that there were a lot of people in the stands. They were talking happily. He knew some of his sister's friends, but not others. Several friends approached Nat, and she amusedly began to chat with them.

Sam looked around but didn't find a single boy his age. For a moment, he didn't feel right there and thought he was out of place. He thought about how well he could be at home now, quiet with his things.

They sat on the bleachers, watching his sister. Mom had a drink in a closed glass and some knickknacks to pass the time.

Nat went to the locker room and, after coming in in uniform, walked onto the court. She was beaming with joy.

The coach was an older gentleman with gray hair and a kindly look. He had a whistle and blew it every moment to guide everyone ordering positions and ways to throw or evade.

Each of the players stood around him and began practice. Separated into teams, the plan was for one to come out on top while the coach corrected them.

Nat, with her friends, was in the yellow jersey group, and the others were in red shirts. They soon realized that one player was missing from the red team. Everyone was worried, as this would affect the whole game.

They discussed and looked for options, but nothing appeared until Nat said something that sounded like a joke but was also serious:

"My brother can play."

There was silence.

Then, more assuredly, she pointed her finger at her brother.

"There he is. We can bring him in to play."

Sam felt himself sink into the chair; his face grew hot, and his heart pounded.

He couldn't believe what he had heard—a boy playing basketball with girls that had never been seen before, or so he thought.

"If your brother feels up to it, he's welcome." said the coach.

They all seemed to agree with what the coach said and were waiting for him to say yes or no.

Sam felt his heart go to the floor and said almost in a whisper:

"Do they really want me to participate?"

"Of course, come; we need you." Nat said.

His mother said:

"The girls don't mind if you participate; go, and maybe you like it. Although it's best if you decide for yourself."

Sam thought about it for a moment. He knew he could do it because he had played with his sister in the house. He knew the rules of the game and had seen many games with his dad and sister.

He knew about throwing the ball in the basket, scoring, and not kicking the ball, as well as the other rules.

Maybe he wouldn't do it like his sister, but he could fill the missing spot.

"Okay, I'm in." he said.

For the first few minutes, there were no baskets scored in the game; both teams were evenly matched and knew how to defend the hoop. The ball was passed back and forth, and the match was thrilling because all the players were well-coached. Suddenly, one of the girls from Sam's team made an error and lost the ball near the basket. Another player seized the opportunity, caught the ball mid-air, and scored.

The team was not to be disheartened by this first score, though, as they were committed and began to even the game, and shortly before the end of the game, they were tied in the score.

It couldn't have been more exciting. The final minutes were challenging. It was time to see who would win and walk off the court proudly.

Nat encouraged her team to continue and felt proud of her brother. He was playing with ambition and a desire to win proving that boys can play too.

He was completely focused and wanted to win. Before the game was over, with just seconds left, the ball fell into his hands, and it was now or never time. It was their chance to score another point. The rivals tried to take the ball away from him, and at that moment, he saw his sister, then smiled at her with

friendly rivalry and moved nimbly down the court, rose up, and saw the basket.

In a clean shot, the ball went into the basket. There was a great silence. Then everyone shouted because it had been missing points to be able to win.

Nat ran to her brother and hugged him, congratulating him on such a good game.

"What a nice, clean shot you made, little brother." She said to him.

He jumped up and down.

"I told you you'd have fun." She said it again.

Sam felt happy and proud of himself. His mother also congratulated him and applauded him. At home, Sam was excited.

"It's been great this day. I didn't think I would have so much fun."

"Too bad there's no boys' basketball," he said.

"Of course there is. There's a boys' league at the club. You can go; they train on Saturdays; shall we go?"

Sam thought it was the best idea ever. He had had a great time that day, and maybe if he tried one day,

he could be in a league, playing in big stadiums, and winning championships.

Dreams are wonderful if you set out to pursue them.

Although he found those games or workouts boring, he had now overcome his fear of trying new things and had a lot of fun.

Leo the Skater

Have you ever wanted to do something new and others laughed at you? It can be very painful, and often we don't try new things because we are afraid of being judged. It can be scary because you don't know what others think, and you don't want to be made fun of. Trying new things takes a lot of courage. Stepping out of our comfort zone to learn something new can be challenging, but it is very rewarding once you do it.

Don't let anyone stop you from doing the things you want to do. Believe in yourself.

At the park, Leo watched three skaters on the rink. They were spinning and gliding along the rink, and Leo couldn't help but think, "I want to be like them," so he walked over and asked them, "Would you mind showing me some tricks?" Leo asked the skaters. The three looked at each other and laughed at Leo. They thought Leo was joking. A little boy like him couldn't do these difficult tricks.

"Go away, little boy; you're not going to be able to do these figures. They're too hard for you," one of them said.

"Yes, go play on the slides," said the other.

Leo walked away and sat on a bench in the park, discouraged and annoyed. He thought the skaters were cool and wanted to be like them, but they were so mean.

That day, Leo walked home with his head down. He didn't know what to do until he looked up and saw a flyer on a pole advertising a big skating competition coming to town, and the winner would get a special prize!

Leo ripped off the poster and ran home to tell his dad.

"Dad, Dad!"

"Hey, Leo, what's up?"

"There's a new skating competition coming to town, and I want to join. Can I buy some skates?"

"Of course, you can, Leo, I can take you now!" his father said.

Leo got in the car with his father, and they drove to the sporting goods store, where there were so many skates and skating equipment.

His eyes looked around the store. "Which ones do you like?" his father asked. Leo was confused by the many types, but then he saw some that caught his eye. They had cool, colorful wheels.

"Those!" Leo pointed them out. And his dad bought some awesome skates for Leo.

"What made you want to do this?" his dad asked him.

Right then, Leo knew he wanted to show the skater boys at the park that he could skate and do any trick like them.

"I want to prove to myself that I can do it," he smiled, picking up his skates.

Later that day, Leo started watching videos so he could study the figures.

He put on his skates and tried to keep his balance, but he was a little unsteady.

"I can do this," he said to himself as he propelled himself and rolled slowly.

"I'm moving! Daddy, look!" Leo yelled to his father from outside. His father gave him a thumbs-up sign and a wide grin.

Leo practiced his balance and pushed himself back and forth across the yard until he could do it without falling. Eventually, he became faster and faster, skating all over the backyard. He would lean from side to side to turn, and backward when he wanted to stop.

Up to this point, Leo could get around riding his skates, but now he needed to take his skills to the park, where he could watch other skaters and learn from them.

He studied them as they glided and made graceful figures. He took notes on how to do it. Finally, he walked out to the rink and saw its immense size.

"It's too big," he said nervously. The skaters looked at him with teasing smiles. They were waiting to see Leo fall.

He started to step forward and continued on the other skate to propel himself, lifted one foot to try to make a figure, and leaned forward.

"Ahhh!" Leo screamed and rolled to the ground.

He scraped his knee but got back up on his skates.

The skaters laughed and walked back to their rink.

"I knew he'd fall," laughed one of them.

But Leo refused to give up. He tried again. Again and again, he fell and got up.

"This is harder than I thought," he said, dusting himself off.

"Don't panic. Be confident and keep your feet steady on your skates," said a boy who was watching Leo in the park.

Leo looked at him and smiled at his words of encouragement. He needed all the advice he could get.

Leo stood on the track to try again. He swallowed saliva and remembered the boy's words. He leaned forward and began to propel himself with the skates. He rolled down the rink, lifting one foot and spinning;

this time, he managed to keep his balance and spun back to the other side without falling.

"I did it. I did it!" Leo ran over to the little boy to give him a high five.

"I'll show you some figures," he said, getting up on his skates. He rolled down the rink, spinning and flipping in the air. Leo watched in amazement. He couldn't believe his eyes and wondered how he could make those kinds of figures.

"It's all about having confidence and making sure you balance your body, and then when you're in the air, you do whatever!"

"I'll try it," said Leo.

This time, with more assurance and confidence, he tried it again. He spun, flipped in the air, and landed on the runway without losing his balance! Leo and the little boy celebrated.

After practicing a bit that day, he returned home, and his father asked him how his practice was.

"I'm going to compete, Dad! A very nice boy at the park helped me, and now I can do some figures. Of course, I need more practice, but I'm sure I can win," Leo said.

His dad hugged him tight; he was proud of Leo for not giving up.

The time came, and it was the day of the competition. Leo's family and friends were there to cheer him on. Leo was practicing before the competition when one of the skater boys from the park approached him.

"You're not going to win with those ugly skates," one said.

Leo turned around.

"I'm going to win because I'm a good skater," Leo asserted.

Of course, they didn't believe him, but that's when Leo proved them wrong.

When it was his turn, he did the unimaginable figures that came out perfectly.

The audience began to applaud and cheer him on. The other contestants skated well, but Leo certainly stole the show.

The moment everyone was waiting for...

"And the winner is Leo!"

He jumps out of his seat. "Yes!"

He ran to receive his prize. They were sleek orange skates with cool designs, some of the best you could get.

His friends and family came running over to give him a big hug. His dad lifted him on his shoulders, and they celebrated.

Leo proved to everyone that you could choose to do something new and practice hard to achieve it.

There were those who didn't believe in him, but he didn't lose confidence and was determined to win. When people don't support us, we should take it as a way to prove them wrong. If he had listened to the skater boys, he wouldn't have been as good on the rink and won the competition.

He used the negative things to push him to do better. When you believe in yourself and don't let anyone get to you, you can achieve greater things.

Bruno's Adventures and Lessons Learned

Do you want to get a new pet? Have you asked your parents for one, and they haven't given it to you yet? This story is about a little boy getting his beloved pet and learning a few lessons.

James wanted a dog for a long time; first, he asked Santa for it, but his parents told him that he didn't

bring living beings because something could happen to them on the sleigh. Then he asked his parents, but they had opposed; they told him not yet, or that it could damage the furniture, dirty inside the house, and even his father said:

"To have a dog is to have one more child."

James did not understand his words because a dog did not look like a human. On the contrary, it was a beautiful little furry thing.

His parents always told him that if he wanted to have a dog, he had to learn a few rules; they told him that he would have to take care of it, take it outside to relieve itself, brush it, bathe it, take it to the vet, feed it, water it, pick up its waste in the street, and take out its dead hair.

Except for picking up litter, everything else seemed very sweet to James. He dreamed of doing it, so much so that with a stuffed dog that his parents gave him, hoping that this would calm his desire for the pet, he brushed him, talked to him, and every time he went out, he put him on a leash so that he would go with him.

But it didn't fill the void that a real dog could fill.

When he was away, the parents discussed the likelihood of having a dog because they knew their son and knew that he only saw the romance of having one, not the consequences and responsibilities. The more practical mother told him:

"I think we should buy him the dog and give it to him; it will serve as a lesson for him to know the responsibilities. Besides, you also want a dog at home, don't you?"

The father smiled. It was true. He wanted a dog.

Meanwhile, James's friend Tom, a neighbor who lived a couple of blocks from his house, had a dog. James told him about his desire to have one, but his parents refused.

"Well, having a dog is nice, although it is a lot of work." His friend told him.

"You say that because you don't love your dog enough."

"What are you saying? I love it! To little flea."

"You gave him that name; I don't think you love him that much."

Tom raised his eyes to the sky.

"I mean, a dog is the best, but it also has responsibilities."

"I'll do it with all the love in the world," he said.

That night, his mother called him from the lower part of the house. So he went downstairs, and in the middle of the room, there was a little closed cardboard box.

James's heart began to pound. He could not believe that what his little eyes were seeing was a probability.

He went a little further and saw his parents looking at him with big smiles.

He knelt, opened the box carefully, and inside was a beautiful Siberian husky dog; it looked like a stuffed animal.

It was love at first sight.

Bruno was the name he baptized him with, and they began to be best friends from the very first moment, although his mother had a document prepared for him.

"Son, these are your responsibilities with the dog, and they are non-negotiable."

James accepted without seeing them; he talked about taking responsibility for the damages, cleaning up every mess, cleaning it up, and everything that involved the dog's care.

The first gift he left shortly after was in the living room. Bruno walked over, opened his hind legs, and peed.

James shuddered a little, but without complaining, he went to the yard, got a rag to wipe the floor and a disinfectant, and cleaned up.

He had to read on the internet in detail how to teach a dog to relieve itself in one place and ask his neighbors for newspapers to remove them from time to time and clean up.

From that first moment, he realized that although the dog was wonderful, it also implied some responsibilities, and he had to assume them.

But James was in the springtime of love with Bruno, so he tidied up quickly, trying to prevent his parents from regretting the acquisition.

He hid the toys that he had eaten in a few bites and the sports shoes that were almost new and destroyed, leaving them in strips.

Weeks went by, and Bruno was growing very fast. He was already quite big, and according to the internet, it was time to teach him to relieve himself outside. However, the first day he took him out, he pulled him by the leash as he took him to do his business; he had not yet educated him to go by his side.

He tried his best as he cleaned up the debris on the floor and then had a hard time doing it to get him in the house.

Days later, he could control the dog better when he took him out, and one day, as he was going out, the key to the front door fell out of his hand. He saw Bruno and said,

"Wait, don't go away."

He let go of his leash to grab the key, and the dog immediately ran off at full speed and took off down the block.

"Bruno!" James said to him, but he was no longer around. Scared, he ran out and had to go several blocks to finally find him in the garden of a house. The owner was outside and yelled at him to go away, but the dog moved from one side to the other and rubbed himself, destroying everything and scattering dirt all over the ground.

"Is it your dog?" he asked.

James nodded.

"I think he gave you a job, you know, gardening?"

James didn't know anything, but he nodded. He was responsible. He had to answer for his dog.

"Besides, you have to take care of that." He showed him a large, fresh, discarded gift she had left by the front door.

"I'll get it, sir."

"Did it get away from you?"

"Yes, sir."

"What a naughty boy he is."

James took the dog home and came back with what he needed to start replenishing the neighbor's garden. He put all the soil in its place and rescued the plants that had not succumbed to Bruno's mischief.

He returned exhausted, his hands burning because some plants have small thorns, and his little hands were not used to handling tools.

When he arrived, he saw Bruno, happy to play with him.

"I understand, my friend. It's nice to have a dog, but they can give you work that the ads don't tell you about. I would never leave you anyway, my naughty madman."

James began to chase Bruno, and he responded with barking and happiness. They were days of learning. For a long time, he had wanted a dog, thinking everything would be joyous, but he had responsibilities.

Little by little, he educated him, taught him the basic commands, and taught him to respect him, making him the leader between the two of them, and he always obeyed him. Thus, his responsibility was to take him out three times a day, give him food, take him to the doctor now and then, and take good care of him, besides filling him with love, which he liked the most.

Pets are beautiful; they bring joy to our lives, but each one has responsibilities, and we must assume them. One has responsibilities, and we must assume them.

Scaling New Heights

Have you ever faced a huge challenge that you were afraid to tackle? Have you been scared to do something that, deep down, you really wanted to do? This story will teach you that when you manage to face what you fear and desire at the same time, you gain achievements that are worth more than just doing them; it leaves you with such a nice feeling that it is hard to describe.

Charlie's mother woke him up excitedly.

"Son, wake up. You have to go now. Your dad is waiting for you."

Charlie knew this was a special day. When he got to the kitchen, after getting cleaned up and dressed, his father at the table greeted him and then said,

"If you waste time like this, you are going to be late."

"Yes, Dad, I'll get up on time tomorrow."

He felt tired and wanted to continue hugging his pillow, sleeping carefree. Although his father was not so strict, he did like order and things to be done right.

His mother made him breakfast, a delicious fruit salad, and yogurt.

While he was eating to go to class, he remembered that he would have a special day, as it would be climbing practice at school.

He had recently started practicing it and liked it. They would take him with a rope and straps around his waist, and he would start climbing a wall to the top. It seemed simple, but it was exhausting.

Normally he liked it, but he had such a full schedule lately that he didn't feel like it as much.

The father noticed something was wrong with Charlie and asked him.

"It's just that today we have to climb more, and even though I like it, I'm afraid to climb so high."

"But you're secured."

"I know and I understand, but the fear of falling is present. Today we will have to climb the highest wall."

"Charlie," said affectionately, "tell your teacher that you are afraid to climb so high, and that's why you won't. I'm sure he'll understand."

Charlie's teacher was knowledgeable and attentive, popular at school, and always positive about education.

Charlie was worried about what people would say.

"But will others make fun of me? Maybe they'll call me a chicken."

The father looked at him fondly, and he continued.

"I really want to climb the highest wall. It must feel good."

"I'll tell you a secret. That way, you'll get over your fear." His father told him.

"But it scares the hell out of me."

Dad paused for a moment, thinking about how he could help Charlie. Then he gently took Charlie's hand and spoke in a soft voice: "I'm going to tell you a secret, or rather a little trick that has always helped me overcome my fear."

His father told him to breathe, to inhale and exhale, and to trust that he would make it that everything was safe.

His words gave him encouragement.

At school, it was time to do the climb. The teacher ordered everyone to put on their protection to start climbing the highest wall.

Charlie anxiously walked to get dressed, and he met Chris, his best friend, who was also getting dressed.

They had been friends since they were little boys and now went to class together. He loved climbing and was good at it.

"You look different today," Chris told him. "Are you afraid?" he said.

He noticed that Charlie was quieter than usual and seemed tense.

They were best friends and usually talked and laughed together when they saw each other. Charlie replied with his head down and his voice unsure, "Well, I'm already a little nervous." A lump formed in his throat.

He pulled himself together and continued speaking, "I have never climbed so high, and, in fact, I'm afraid of heights."

Charlie was glad he could talk to Chris about anything. He was his best friend and would never laugh at him.

"Oh, you're going to be fine."

"Stop thinking so much," he told him when Charlie nodded.

"Besides, I'll be with you."

After everyone had changed into their climbing safety gear, Charlie saw that wall higher than ever.

His legs began to tremble, and he suddenly felt the air go out of him. His friend, who was standing next to him, leaned out and encouraged him.

"I know you can do it; we'll both do it."

Charlie was relieved to have his friend supporting him again.

The first to climb was Joseph, who did it in no time, and everyone applauded him, proudly watching his accomplishment from above.

Although everyone was doing it carefully and putting their foot on each rung, they were careful not to fall. Some slipped and tried again. Others did better with practice, and when it was Chris's turn, he did it fast, climbing with alacrity and concentrating on each movement of his limbs.

It was Charlie's turn, who, with fear, thought that the others had done it, and it looked easy. It was just a matter of concentrating and trying. His heart was pounding, and his legs felt like rubber. But Charlie walked slowly; he wanted to turn back, but deep down, the voice told him to do it and that he could.

He remembered what his father told him at the last moment about breathing. He did it three times, deep, and closed his eyes as he touched the first obstacle and his feet left the ground.

Then he went up step by step, concentrating on what his hands were holding and where his feet were resting, being careful that each limb was well

supported to move hand, foot, and whatever he was moving up.

Everything was silent; he felt powerful, and each step was a small achievement. He succeeded, and this filled him with great happiness. If he had not dared to climb to the top, he would not be so proud of himself. He climbed down, and everyone congratulated him and looked at him with pride.

Chris saw him with a smile and said to him:

"I was sure you would make it. It wasn't that hard, as you could see."

Then the children were able to entertain themselves with other things in the classroom, but the big challenge of the climbing had been overcome without a problem.

When he returned home, Charlie looked forward to telling his father how he had done. He was excited and proud.

"Your advice helped me a lot, Dad. Thank you." He said that and gave him a kiss on the cheek.

"You did a great job, son. I'm proud of you. Do you know how much I love you?"

Charlie nodded his head.

The two embraced.

That night, when he went to bed, his father kissed him goodnight as he did every day and then turned out the light.

Charlie that day lay in bed for a while, awake, with many emotions inside; he wasn't able to sleep because it had been a day he would never forget.

He learned that he could do whatever he set his mind to if he believed in himself; his great fear he had been able to overcome, and now he was full of satisfaction and happiness. Finally, he fell asleep.

When you believe in yourself and face your fears, no matter how big they may be, you achieve your dreams.

The Betrayed Secret

Have you ever known a secret about someone you care about? Did you ever tell someone else? Secrets can sometimes lead to big adventures. This story is about a brother who shared his sibling's secret.

During the summer months, Matthew had a great time. During that time, he finally learned to stop with his skateboard; he also made a new friend who he felt would be for his lifetime; he fell and scraped his

elbow, took a week to heal, went to a heated pool he had never tried before, and spent a lot of time with his new friend and others he already had. Every day, enjoy playing and living childhood to the fullest. Without school, homework, and just being happy, vacations were the best for him. It was also the time he discovered that his brother Sam had a diary hidden under the mattress and began to read it.

The day he found that diary, at first he took it, but he immediately let it go and left it there as if he had touched a snake. Maybe if his brother had been at home, he would not have touched it again, but since he was not, he had gone to see a friend and would not return for hours. He took it determinedly.

Matthew's brother went to the city to visit a close friend. They planned to play video games and might even have a sleepover because they were such good buddies. Matthew felt a twinge of jealousy. While his brother was having so much fun in the city, he was at home with his nearby friends. He wished his brother would stay home more. They could dust off the old video game console and play together. Sometimes, Matthew wondered if his brother didn't enjoy playing with him as much as with others.

He sat on his brother's bed, put his pillow on his legs, and adjusted it until he felt quite comfortable. There

he had in his hands that blue diary with a cool car on the cover. He looked at it for a while and thought about whether to open it or not. For long seconds, he was thinking about whether or not to take that step into his brother's universe and get to know it. Then, after thinking about it and making excuses for his brother, accusing him of things he had never done, he finally began to flip through the pages.

He was already sailing through Sam's intimate universe, seeing things he didn't know about him and reading line by line with great dedication.

Although while he was reading it, he felt a little disappointed, as he was hoping to find more exciting and complex things from his brother. There were only topics about the homework he had turned in, recipes he would never make because they wouldn't let him cook, video game cheats, making promises to himself to buy things at the comic convention that year, and things like that.

Although he was showing a face that his brother didn't know, the truth was that there wasn't much gossip-worthy information in the diary—nothing at all. But finally, on July 1st, he came across something that made his eyes widen.

In the words he found, it said something like, "I like Lucy." Just as he read that, he knew he shouldn't have. This was a huge secret that he didn't know, and Sam had probably only shared it with his diary and no one else. Matthew got up, put the pillow back where it was, and went to his room. He started reading more there. He didn't tell his brother anything. All he did was try to forget what he had read.

He tried to forget about that diary completely; for a few weeks, he didn't think about it, but then it came back to his mind. It was one of those summer days when you started thinking about going back to school because the days are long and boring, and there's not much to do. While killing time, the diary came back to his mind, and again, Sam's intimate declaration about his feelings for Lucy.

For some unimportant reason, as many arguments began, Matthew started fighting with Sam, and things became more intense, and each one said something worse to the other until it got worse, and Sam started crying, hurt, and saying something mean to Matthew, and he also ended up crying. Sam, feeling frustrated, left and left him there, alone and feeling like he had lost the argument.

When Matthew had vented and wiped away each of his tears, he knew he had something in mind that he would put into action as soon as possible, as it was a severe wrong, but just what his brother had done to him. He was tired of losing the argument every time he fought with Sam. So he took Sam's diary out of the room and told his mom he was going to play with a friend for a while.

He walked and arrived at Luke's house, one of his best friends. He showed him the diary with confidence, like the gossip of the month or year. They turned the pages until they reached the part where he had declared that he liked Lucy and also showed him what he had written below with a heart, an "I love you," and the initials "S & L." After this, he went home to tell Sam what he had done.

The brother, who had already forgotten about the argument, turned pale when he saw the diary in Matthew's hands and even paler when he found out what he had done. He also told him that Luke had called him a loser for being into having a diary and wanting to like the prettiest girl in school.

What Matthew wanted was for his brother to start crying, to see him heartbroken, just as he always ended up.

Matthew doesn't remember the reason for the fight, but what stuck with him forever was Sam's face when he realized everything Matthew had done—that look of disappointment and sadness for the betrayal. It was a horrible memory because one thing was to fight over something silly, and another was to show something as intimate as the diary and make his brother look ridiculous.

Although Sam started crying, they were tears of humiliation, pain, and anger. Matthew didn't feel like a winner. He felt worse than ever. The shame of having his brother's most private secrets and divulging them—something that would surely be the gossip of the whole neighborhood

It was a tough lesson he had to learn.

Never divulge the secrets of the people you love, no matter how angry you are.

82065873R00046